WHERE IS THE POKY LITTLE PUPPY?

By JANETTE SEBRING LOWREY
Illustrated by GUSTAF TENGGREN

g A GOLDEN BOOK • NEW YORK

Somebody left the gate open one morning, and five little puppies went scampering through as fast as their legs would carry them.

Down the lane they went, under the fence, past the beehives, and up to the edge of the pond.

One, two, three, four little puppies; one little puppy wasn't there.

"Now where in the world is that poky little puppy?" they wondered. For he certainly wasn't sitting on the edge of the pond.

He wasn't swimming in the water. The only thing swimming in the water was a greeny-gray turtle.

He wasn't in the leafy tree. The only thing chirping in the leafy tree was a Katydid.

But when they sat still and listened, they could hear a faraway sound.

"What-what-what? What-what-what?" the poky little puppy was saying far away.

"What in the world is he talking about?" wondered the four little puppies. And away they went to find out, hippity-hoppity, higgledy-piggledy, head-over-heels.

And they found that poky little puppy in the middle of the road, talking to an old rubber boot.

"What are you talking about?" they asked him.

"This is a very fine rubber boot," said the poky little puppy. "This is the very finest, largest, emptiest rubber boot in the whole round world!"

"We'll take it home for you," said the four little puppies. And so they did, push-pull, huff-puff, all the way home, and left the boot on the front lawn for the poky little puppy to play with.

Their mother didn't like it one bit.

"What is that old rubber boot doing on my nice green grass?" she said. "It's bedtime. Come eat your bread and milk."

And by the time the poky puppy got there, the rubber boot was gone and he went to bed feeling most forlorn.

The next morning, there was a notice on the gate. It said:

RULE ONE :
DON'T BRING THINGS IN HERE

BUT somebody had left the gate ajar, and five little puppies went scampering through again, as fast as their legs would carry them.

Down the lane they went, under the fence, and up to the beehives. One, two, three, four little puppies. One little puppy wasn't there.

"Now where in the world is that poky little puppy?" they wondered. For he certainly wasn't near the beehives.

He wasn't in the thornbush. The only thing in the thornbush was a bee bird building a nest.

He wasn't in the wildflowers. The only things buzzing around the wildflowers were six golden bees. But when they sat still and listened, they could hear a faraway sound. "Ow-ooh-ooh!" the poky little puppy was saying far away.

"What in the world is he howling about?" they wondered. And away they went to find out, hippity-hoppity, higgledy-piggledy, head-over-heels. And they found the poky little puppy in the middle of the road, howling at the top of his voice.

"What is the matter with you?" they asked him.

"Ow-ooh-ooh! I can't find my rubber boot!" said the poky little puppy. "Ow-ooh-ooh!"

"We'll find it for you," they said.

And away they went, to rummage in all sorts of places, until each one found a shoe: a shoe with strings, a shoe with straps, a shoe with buttons, and a baby's shoe. They took the four shoes home, hugger-mugger, huff-puff, and left them on the front lawn.

(Four shoes! Dear me, that ought to please him!)

Their mother was upset, to say the least.

"Will you kindly stop cluttering up my nice green grass with old shoes and things?" she said. "It's bedtime. Come and eat your bread and milk."

The poky puppy found the four shoes waiting for him when he came home, but there wasn't a rubber boot among them, and so he went to bed as miserable as ever.

And the next morning there was another notice on the gate. It said:

RULE TWO : DON'T YOU DARE BRING THINGS IN HERE AGAIN !

But somebody had left the gate off the latch, as usual, and five little puppies went scampering through as fast as their legs could carry them.

Down the lane they went and up to the fence. One, two, three, four little puppies. One little puppy wasn't there.

"Now where in the world is that poky little puppy?" they wondered. For he certainly wasn't on this side of the fence.

He hadn't crawled under the fence. The
only thing on the other side of the fence was
a bushy-tailed squirrel.

He wasn't down a rabbit hole. The only thing
peeping out of the rabbit hole was a scared rabbit.

But when they sat still and listened, they could hear a voice far away. It sounded like somebody crying.

"Now what in the world is that poky puppy yapping about?" they wondered. And away they went to find out, hippity-hoppity, higgledy-piggledy, head-over-heels, till they found the poky little puppy, his head on his paws, crying quietly to himself.

"We'll just have to find that rubber boot for him," they said.

They spent half the day rummaging in all sorts
of places till they found dozens of shoes, and they
dragged them all home, push-pull, hugger-mugger,
huff-puff, and piled them up on the front lawn.
(There wasn't a rubber boot in the lot. Oh, dear!)

And their mother was beside herself.

"My heart is broken!" she cried. "Just look at my
nice green grass!"

"We'll take them back again," said the four little puppies. "Anyway, we didn't find that rubber boot." And so they spent the rest of the day taking the shoes back, and when they were through, their mother was very pleased with them.

"Such good little puppies!" she said. "Come and have some ice-cream and cake and fried chicken and rice and gravy. And is it an old rubber boot you've been hunting? Well, just look under the morning-glory vines and see if it's not there."

The four little puppies looked under the morning-glory vines, and there it was, the old rubber boot that the poky puppy liked so much. They dragged it out so he could see it.

While they were eating their good dinner, the poky little puppy came home.

"What a pity you're so poky!" said his mother. "If you had come home with the others that day, I would have known you liked that rubber boot and I wouldn't have put it away. There it is now. But you must eat your dinner first."

So the poky little puppy ate his fried
chicken and ice-cream as fast as he could
and then he ran over to that old rubber boot,
crawled inside it, and slept there the whole
night through, just as happy as a lark.

And the next morning, there was a notice hanging on the gate. It said:

RULE THREE:
NEVER EVER BRING THINGS
IN HERE AGAIN.

(IF YOU WANT TO KEEP THAT OLD RUBBER BOOT.)